Sakes Alive!
A Cattle Drive

by

Karma Wilson

Illustrated by

Karla Firehammer

Megan Tingley Books
LITTLE, BROWN AND COMPANY
New York · Boston

To my wonderful mom, Shelly Marshall,
whom I drove up a wall more than once.

Love, K.W.

For Mark, Zach, and Josh

—K.F.

Little, Brown and Company

Time Warner Book Group
1271 Avenue of the Americas, New York, NY 10020
Visit our Web site at www.lb-kids.com

First Edition

ISBN 0-316-98841-3
LCCN: 2004106357

10 9 8 7 6 5 4 3 2 1

TWP

Printed in Singapore

The illustrations for this book were done in acrylics on Strathmore board.
The text was set in Carré Noir Light, and the display type is Linotype Tapeside.

One day . . .

the cows took Farmer's keys
right from his back pocket.

They tippy-toed to Farmer's truck
and hurried to unlock it.

Molly revved the engine up,
then rolled the windows down.
And Mabel waved to Farmer
as they zoomed away to town.

The farmer shouted,

"Sakes alive!

They're going on a cattle drive!"

They bounced along the bumpy road
at quite a frightful speed.

"What's that sign say?" Mabel asked.
But cows, of course, can't read.

Molly swerved to miss a car.
She dodged it just in time!
Mabel cried, "How some folks drive
should surely be a crime!"

The sheriff shouted,

**"Sakes alive!
Did I just see those cattle drive?"**

The sheriff flipped his siren on
and whipped his car around.
Mabel mooed, "I do-o-o declare,
what is that awful sound?"

Molly shrugged. "I couldn't say.
A flock of noisy geese?"
Meanwhile Sheriff hollered out,

**"PULL OVER!
STOP!
POLICE!"**

He called for backup.

"Sakes alive! We've got to stop this cattle drive!"

His deputy said, "Are you *sure*?
Since when do cattle drive?"
Sheriff yelled, "Well these ones can.
They're going eighty-five!"

Three police cars joined the chase.
"Mabel, look!" said Molly.
"Those cars have pretty flashing lights!"
And Mabel said, "Good golly!"

The deputy cried,

"Sakes alive!
It really IS a cattle drive!"

Mabel pointed up ahead.
"I do-o-o believe that's town!"
Molly uttered, "Where're the brakes?
HELP! I can't slow down!"

They whizzed right past the firehouse;
the chief yelled, "HOLY COW!
They're headed for the mayor's place!
Let's stop those cattle now!"

The firemen screamed,

"Sakes alive!
Mayor, move! A cattle drive!"

They sideswiped
    Mayor's flower bed.

They barely missed
    his garden shed.

The mayor shook
his fists and said,

"Cattle shouldn't drive!"

They roared through town;
the sirens blared.
The townsfolk gathered
round and stared.

"A town parade!"
they all declared . . .

"Watch those cattle drive!"

"Turn the key off!"
Mabel cried.
The pickup slowed.
The engine died.
    Molly fainted.
        Mabel sighed,

    "Next time let me drive . . ."

The truck stopped by the city jail.
The crowd began to cheer!
"The best parade we've ever seen!
Let's do this every year!"

The people wanted autographs,
but cows, of course, can't spell.
They stamped their hooves in pads of ink,
which worked out rather well.

The mayor muttered,

"Sakes alive!
The whole town loves this cattle drive!"

The farmer galloped into town.
He had to ride his horse.

The sheriff asked, "Are these your cows?"
And Farmer said, "Of course!"

"Come on, cows, we'd best get home.
Dinner's on the table."
The horse neighed, "Farmer, may I drive?"
And Molly looked at Mabel.

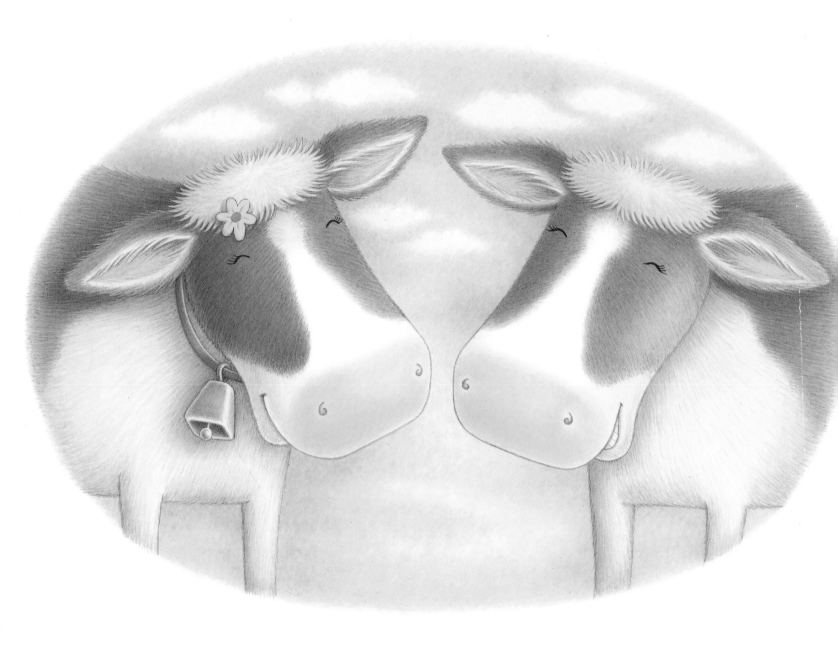

Those cows both giggled.

"Sakes alive!
Since when have you seen HORSES drive?"